MW00910150

Bunny's BIG Surprise

Phyllis Limbacher Tildes

Charlesbridge

For Heather, Jeff, and William,
with love and bunny hugs

Copyright © 2020 by Phyllis Limbacher Tildes
All rights reserved, including the right of reproduction in whole or in part in any form.
   Charlesbridge and colophon are registered trademarks of Charlesbridge Publishing, Inc.

At the time of publication, all URLs printed in this book were accurate and active. Charlesbridge
   and the author are not responsible for the content or accessibility of any website.

Published by Charlesbridge, 85 Main Street, Watertown, MA 02472
   (617) 926-0329 • www.charlesbridge.com

Library of Congress Cataloging-in-Publication Data
Names: Tildes, Phyllis Limbacher, author, illustrator.
Title: Bunny's big surprise / Phyllis Limbacher Tildes.
Description: Watertown, Juvenile fiction. | Eggs--Juvenile fiction. |
   Alligators—Juvenile fiction. | CYAC: Rabbits—Fiction. | Eggs—Fiction. |
   Easter eggs—Fiction. | Alligators—Fiction. | Easter—Fiction. |
   LCGFT: Picture books.
Identifiers: LCCN 2018058508 (print) | LCCN 2018060843 (ebook) |
   ISBN 9781632898302 (ebook) | ISBN 9781632898319 (ebook pdf) |
   ISBN 9781580896849 (reinforced for library use)
Classification: LCC PZ7.T4559 (ebook) | LCC PZ7.T4559 Bu 2020 (print) |
   DDC [E]—dc23
LC record available at https://lccn.loc.gov/2018058508

Printed in China
(hc) 10 9 8 7 6 5 4 3 2 1

Illustrations done in watercolor on 140lb Fabriano paper
Display type set in Wanderlust Decorative and Wanderlust Caps by
   Cultivated Mind
Text type set in Grenadine by MVB Fonts
Color separations by Colourscan Print Co Pte Ltd, Singapore
Printed by 1010 Printing International Limited in Huizhou, Guangdong, China
Production supervision by Brian G. Walker
Designed by Susan Mallory Sherman

One day Bunny found a big egg at the water's edge. He put it in his Easter basket. The egg barely fit next to Bunny's clover, carrots, and paints.

First, Bunny asked Goose, "Is this your egg?"

"I'm afraid not," Goose said, and waddled away.

Next, Bunny asked Heron, "Is this your egg?"
"Never seen it before," Heron said, and waded away.

Finally, Bunny asked Osprey, "Is this your egg?"
"Not mine," answered Osprey, and flew away.

Since it wasn't anyone's egg, Bunny took it home.
"I'll decorate it for Easter," he said.
First, Bunny painted the egg many colors.

He put the big egg in the sun to dry.
All the while, Bunny wondered what could be
inside that big egg.

Soon, Bunny settled down for an afternoon nap.
He drifted off to dream.
In Bunny's dream, the egg . . .

wasn't a gosling,

or a heron chick,

or an osprey chick.

In his dream, the egg hatched
two little Easter chicks!

Tap-tap-tap!
Bunny woke up to tapping sounds.
Something *inside* the big Easter egg
was making noise!

A tiny crack appeared.
The crack got bigger and bigger, until . . .

...the egg cracked all the way open!
Big yellow eyes and a short smiling snout peeked
out at Bunny.

The eyes did not look like the eyes of an Easter chick.
The snout did not look like the
beak of an Easter chick.

The strange little critter crawled out of its shell and onto Bunny's lap. Bunny looked very surprised! The critter opened its mouth.
"*Squeak, squeak, squeak.*"

"You must be hungry," said Bunny.
Bunny picked some fresh clover,
but the little critter would not eat.

Bunny offered it a carrot, but
it still would not eat.

Bunny put the little critter in his Easter basket.
He hopped back to where he had found the egg.

Bunny jumped back!

Close to the water's edge, a mother
alligator opened her mouth.
Four little alligators began to climb
inside—

...and Bunny's little critter jumped out of the basket!

The mother alligator gently closed her mouth and swam away with her *five* babies.

"Oh my," Bunny said. "All along I had . . .

". . . an Easter ALLIGATOR!"